My book is dedicated to Maleehah Zaman (Milli), my sister, who would have been 21 on 3 September 2020.

Amber Zaman

Author: Amber Zaman
Illustrators: Amber Zaman and Ursula Hurst
Copyright Poems & Pictures Ltd
The moral right of author/illustrator has been asserted. All rights reserved.

First Edition - 2020

A CIP catalogues record of the publication is available from the British Library.
ISBN: 9781916254268
Published by Poems & Pictures Ltd
www.poemsandpicturespublishing.org
Editor: Rebecca Thomas, RM Language Services.
Printed in the UK.

My Lockdown Poems

Covid-19 part 1

Covid-19 I do not like you.
Please just go away!
Do not come back,
Not even another day.
You are ruining families,
Taking loved ones and friends.
Please leave my family alone.
I need them here when this all ends.

School

No to school,
No to education,
No to lessons,
And using our imagination.
No to waving goodbye to my parents at the school gates.
No to snacks and pizza on plastic plates.
No to seeing my friends
In the classroom or playground.
No to swim club, football or dancing around.

Keyworker children can go to school.
For them it's a slightly different rule,
But only if they cannot be cared for at home.
Then they are better at school and not alone.
Shielding children must stay inside.
Well away from the virus, they must hide.
The phased re-opening of schools is put on hold.
A government statement that was just too bold.
Two… metres… apart… what is going on?
School paused, homeschooling instead,
my routine totally gone.

Hand sanitiser

Help!
There is no hand sanitiser in the shops or
anywhere.
Help!
This is a pandemic not just a minor scare.
Online outlets do not have any.
I don't know where to try.
Everyone is struggling.
It just makes me want to cry.
Manufacturers are battling to keep up with the
increase in demand:
Millions of people wanting a drop to sanitise
each hand.
Help!
There is no hand sanitiser.

Safety

Dear customers and friends.
We are closed at present.
The situation is very unpleasant.
We really don't know what to do.
We just have to sit at home like you.
From the smallest shop to the biggest fast
food chain,
We do not know when we will open again.
It could be next week, next month or next
year,
But we simply cannot open when we all live in
fear.
For now we are closed.
Just closed.

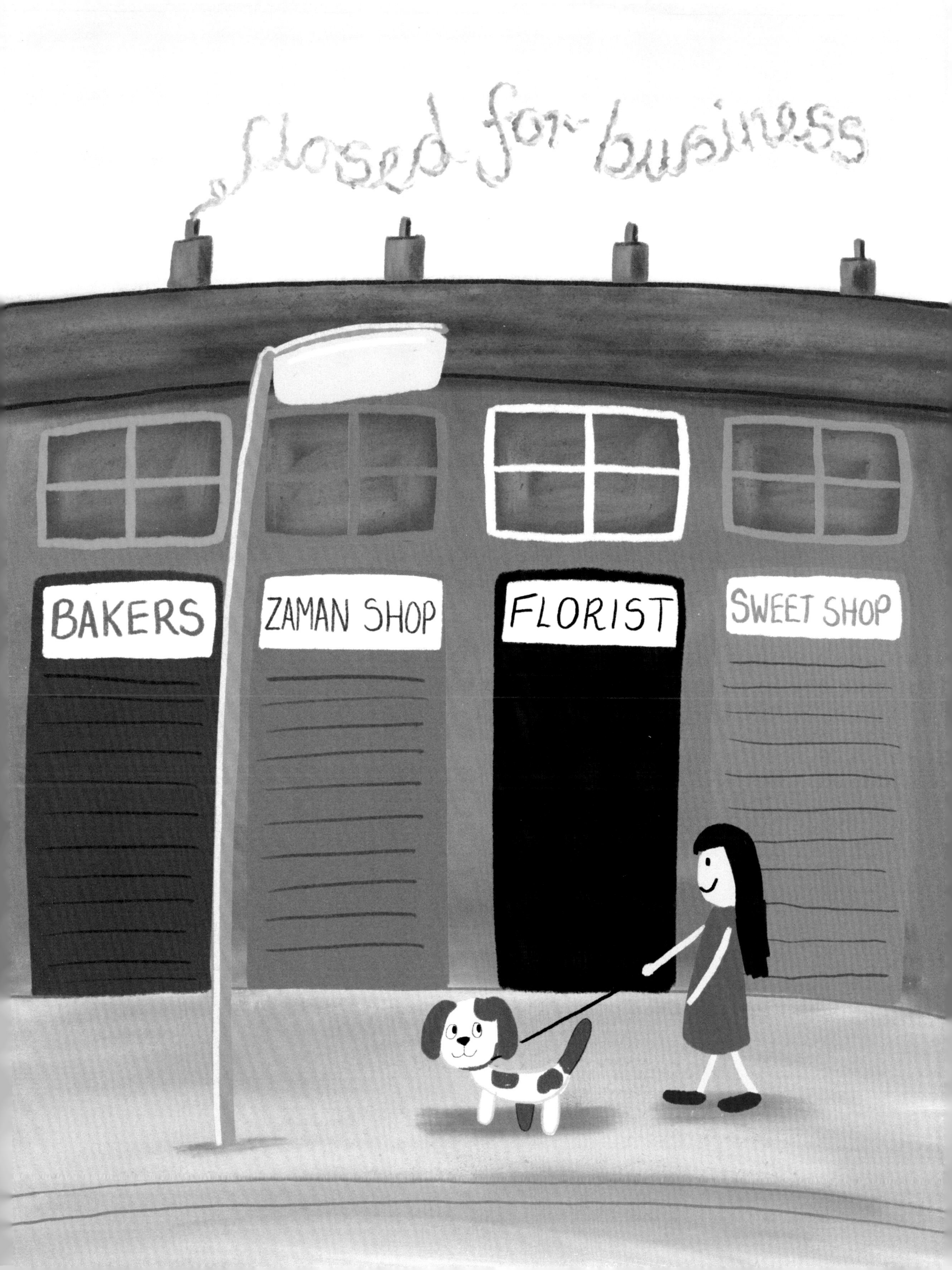
closed for business
BAKERS
ZAMAN SHOP
FLORIST
SWEET SHOP

Covid-19 part 2

Covid-19 what are you
and where did you come from?
I hope you do not intend to stay here very long.
We have to wash our hands all of the time,
And wait to go in shops in a distanced line.
If I have a cough, a temperature,
or lose my sense of smell,
I have to isolate for 14 days
even if I don't feel unwell.
Oh Covid-19 just go away!
Please say you haven't come to stay.

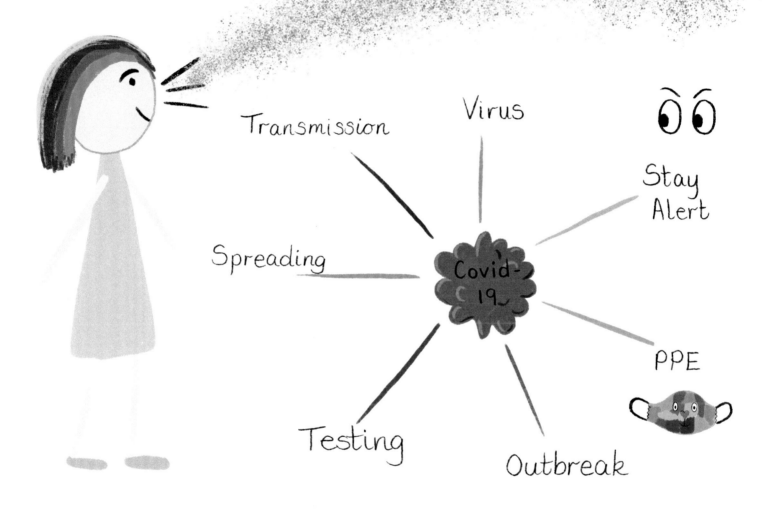

Rainbow

Red, orange, indigo and green,
violet, blue and yellow.
I see you from my window,
The beautiful colours of a rainbow.
Bring on a smile through the rays of the bow.
Now let's thank the NHS,

We all say so,
And the frontline workers for being on the go.
All the colours I simply know.
Red, orange, indigo and green,
violet, blue and yellow:
The beautiful colours of the rainbow.

"Hi, how is lockdown for you?"
"Fine, thanks for asking."
"Ok, call me tomorrow."
Zoom
Time

<u>Technology</u>

Watching our videos on YouTube,
Or following the link for Zoom,
Each conversation a window
into someone else's living room.
FaceTime me,
Message me,
Call me,
Just stay in touch.
We have the technology,
But am I using it too much?
Senseless orders delivered by Amazon and eBay,
An endless stream day by day.
We got this together.
It's the way it's got to be.
Just you and me,
Oh, and technology!

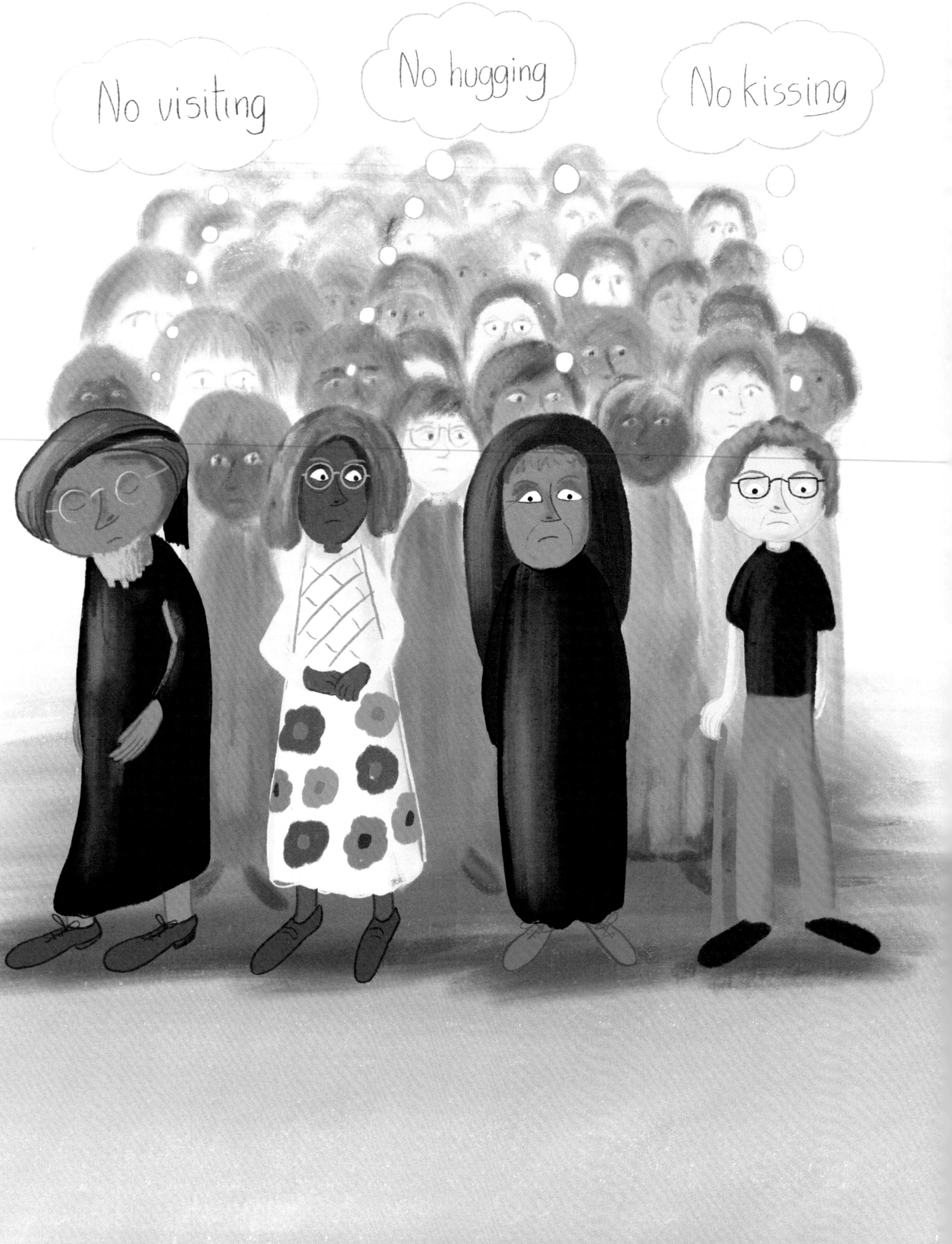
No visiting
No hugging
No kissing

Grandparents

To all the grandparents.
I know it's hard for you.
It's also hard for me too.
No visits, no hugs, and no kisses to be found.
It feels so strange not having you around.
Hang on in there,
It shouldn't be long!
No hugs and kisses will soon be gone.

I love Eid

Feeling closer to Allah, I love Eid.
It is a time of joy indeed.
Lots of presents, and lots of money,
Lots of food that tastes so scrummy.
Lots of embraces and love to make me smile.
It's a time to celebrate for a while.
We have been waiting all year for this day.
We can't wait for the festivities to get underway.
The last thirty days of fasting with no water, no food,
Dry mouth and empty stomach affecting my mood.
But this year we will have to change our plan,
No visiting family and friends, or hugging gran.
But it's ok; I can wait
To be with them and celebrate.
Seeing them again will be so sweet
When we are at last allowed to meet.

Lockdown life with my family

My lockdown birthday inside these four walls,
But instead of people visiting,
it was just phone calls.
My sister and my brother's birthdays both in
lockdown too.
Even my cat Milo, this year wasn't the same for you.
All the celebrations took place in the same room,
Whilst we wait for life to one day resume.

Other activities to fill endless days,
Like making videos for TikTok, the latest craze.
Homework, games or FaceTime with my friends,
Daily decisions, it all depends.
We are allowed to exercise once a day
That is what the government say.
One day things will be normal, it will all change.
Until then life just feels extremely strange.

Covid-19 part 3

Now Covid-19, you are not welcome.
You have been here long enough.
You have caused chaos and disruption,
You have made things very tough.
Businesses are struggling,
Masks and PPE are now the norm.
Life has been changed forever.
We await the end of the storm.

Amber Zaman - Author/Illustrator

Eight-year-old Amber from Yorkshire has wanted to write and illustrate her own book for over a year now. Her dream has finally come true with this, her first publication. Her dream was inspired by her mum being an author and also having other authors, as well as illustrators and editors, among family friends. During lockdown, Amber used poetry and illustration as a means of expressing how she felt about what was happening, developing eleven poems that capture her life during the first four months of the UK's Covid-19 lockdown, alongside illustrations that show a wish for a brighter future. Amber hopes that you will enjoy reading **My Lockdown Poems** and that her book will also inspire other children to read, write and draw, just like she has.

Happy Reading, Writing and Drawing!

Ursula Hurst - Illustrator

Ursula is an illustrator, specialising in children's book illustrations, based in Lancashire.
When she's not drawing on her iPad with her scruffy dog at her feet, she can be found in schools running art workshops, coordinating community festivals, or up a ladder painting murals.

For further information Ursula can be contacted at:

www.artdaze.co.uk

The illustrations

All the illustrations in this book were created in an exciting collaborative way. Amber sent her beautiful drawings to Ursula who used them as inspiration for the final illustrations, creating artwork that looks professional yet maintains the freshness and innocence of Amber's work.
Above you can see an example of how this worked.